FUNNY BUNNY JOKES

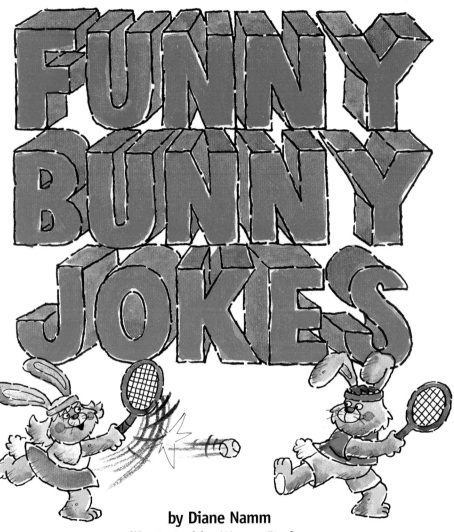

by Diane Namm
illustrated by Wayne Becker

STERLING

New York / London
www.sterlingpublishing.com/kids

STERLING and the distinctive Sterling logo are registered trademarks of
Sterling Publishing Co., Inc.
Library of Congress Cataloging-in-Publication Data

Namm, Diane.
Funny bunny jokes / by Diane Namm, illustrated by Wayne Becker.
p. cm. -- (Laugh-a-long readers)
ISBN-13: 978-1-4027-5634-4
ISBN-10: 1-4027-5634-8
1. Rabbits--Juvenile humor. I. Becker, Wayne. II. Title.
PN6231.R23N36 2008
818'.5402--dc22
2007030250

2 4 6 8 10 9 7 5 3 1

Published and © 2008 by Sterling Publishing Co., Inc.
387 Park Avenue South, New York, NY 10016
Distributed in Canada by Sterling Publishing
c/o Canadian Manda Group, 165 Dufferin Street
Toronto, Ontario, Canada M6K 3H6
Distributed in the United Kingdom by GMC Distribution Services
Castle Place, 166 High Street, Lewes, East Sussex, England BN7 1XU
Distributed in Australia by Capricorn Link (Australia) Pty. Ltd.
P.O. Box 704, Windsor, NSW 2756, Australia

Printed in China

Sterling ISBN-13: 978-1-4027-5634-4
ISBN-10:1-4027-5634-8

For information about custom editions, special sales, premium and
corporate purchases, please contact Sterling Special Sales
Department at 800-805-5489 or specialsales@sterlingpublishing.com.

How do bunnies travel on vacation?

By hare-plane!

Where do bunnies go after they get married?

They go on a bunny-moon.

What's a bunny's favorite music?

Hip-hop!

What do you call a laughing bunny?

"Hoppy!"

What do you get when you cross a bunny with a bee?

You get a honey bunny.

How does the Easter Bunny
stay in shape?

He egg-cercises!

How do bunnies celebrate their birthdays?

With a "Hoppy Birthday" cake.

Why did the bunny eat a gold ring?

He heard it was 18 carrots!

What's blue and has floppy ears?

A bunny at the North Pole.

What do you do when you find
a blue bunny?

Cheer him up.

What's furry, pretty and wears glass slippers?

Cinder-rabbit.

What do you call a bunny in a cereal box?

Stuck!

What's the best way to catch a wild rabbit?

*Stand in the woods
and act like a carrot.*

What do you do if a bunny eats your pen?

Use a pencil.

What did the bunny say
to the bunch of carrots?

It's been nice gnawing you!